Sucked through a worm-hole ...

to a strange, new place,

...ost in a galaxy called Fairy Tale Space.

"What's that bear doing there?"
says Scout.

SCOUT and ACE

The Scary Bear

Written by Rose Impey
Illustrated by Ant Parker

Once upon a time, our heroes,

set out on a trip

into outer, outer-space.

Ace doesn't know, but he says,
"Let's find out."

They fly closer to the bear.

A bit too close!

The bear lives in the barrel,
floating in space.
But he's bored with his barrel.

Scout and Ace feel sorry
for the bear.

They invite him onto their spaceship. Just for a visit.

The bear has never been on
a spaceship before.

But he's soon bored with that, too.

"Grrr!" The bear grumbles and groans.
"It's not fair! *I* want a chair," he moans.

Ace lets the bear have *his* chair.
The bear likes to get his
own way.

Scout tells Ace, "Don't worry.
It's only for today."

But the bear is bored again.
Next he wants Scout's chair.

. . . he gets his own way.

Ace tells Scout, "Don't worry.
It's only for today."

Once the bear has got Scout's chair, he wants to do Scout's job too.

But *he's* never steered a spaceship . . .

. . . and he doesn't have clue.

Scout and Ace feel as if the bear has hijacked the SuperStar.

"We have to get rid of that bear," Ace tells Scout.
But how are they going to get him out?

Soon the bear is bored again.

He tells Scout and Ace he is bored with being Captain. He wants to be King of Space.

At last Scout and Ace have
a plan.

"We have got a throne," says Ace, with a grin on his face.
"Would your highness like to try it out?" asks Scout.

They sit him in the ejector seat.
And they give the bear a crown.

When the bear is sitting
comfortably, Ace pulls the
handle down.

Scout and Ace are free of the bear. Now they can get the SuperStar back on track.

"What did the scary bear take on his trip?" asks Ace. "All the bare essentials! Boom! Boom!"

Scout groans. "Must be time to get out of here," he moans.

Fire the engines...

and lower the dome.

Once more our heroes...

are heading for home.

Enjoy all these stories about

SCOUT and ACE

and their adventures in Space

Scout and Ace: Kippers for Supper
1 84362 172 X

Scout and Ace: Flying in a Frying Pan
1 84362 171 1

Scout and Ace: Stuck on Planet Gloo
1 84362 173 8

Scout and Ace: Kissing Frogs
1 84362 176 2

Scout and Ace: Talking Tables
1 84362 174 6

Scout and Ace: A Cat, a Rat and a Bat
1 84362 175 4

Scout and Ace: Three Heads to Feed
1 84362 177 0

Scout and Ace: The Scary Bear
1 84362 178 9

All priced at £4.99 each.

Colour Crunchies are available from all good bookshops, or can be ordered direct from the publisher:
Orchard Books, PO BOX 29, Douglas MM99 1BQ.
Credit card orders please telephone 01624 836000 or fax 01624 837033
or email: bookshop@enterprise.net for details.

To order please quote title, author and ISBN and your full name and address. Cheques and postal
orders should be made payable to 'Bookpost plc'. Postage and packing is FREE within the UK –
overseas customers should add £1.00 per book. Prices and availability are subject to change.

ORCHARD BOOKS, 96 Leonard Street, London EC2A 4XD.
Hachette Children's Books, Level 17/207 Kent Street, Sydney, NSW 2000.
This edition first published in Great Britain in hardback in 2005. First paperback publication 2006.
Text © Rose Impey 2004. Illustrations © Ant Parker 2005. The rights of Rose Impey to be identified as
the author and Ant Parker to be identified as the illustrator have been asserted by them in accordance with the
Copyright, Designs and Patents Act, 1988. A CIP catalogue record for this book is available from the British Library.
ISBN 1 84362 178 9   10 9 8 7 6 5 4 3 2
Printed in China